D1489376

THIS CANDLEWICK BOOK BELONGS TO:

_____

_____

_____

_____

To Mairi Hedderwick with love
D.G.

For Hannah and Benji
K.S.

Text copyright © 1994 by Debi Gliori
Illustrations copyright © 1994 by Kate Simpson

First U.S. edition 1995
First published in Great Britain in 1994 by Walker Books Ltd., London.

Library of Congress Cataloging-in-Publication Data

Gliori, Debi.
A present for Big Pig / Debi Gliori ; illustrated by
Kate Simpson.—1st U.S. ed.
"First published in Great Britain in 1994 by Walker Books Ltd.,
London"—T.p. verso.
Summary: Little Pig has a present for Big Pig but
can't seem to get it wrapped without entangling himself
and all his animal friends in paper and sticky tape.
ISBN 1-56402-460-1
[1. Pigs—Fiction.  2. Animals—Fiction.  3. Gifts—Fiction.
4. Helpfulness—Fiction.]  I. Simpson, Kate, ill.  II. Title.
PZ7.G4889Pr    1995
[E]—dc20        93-40491

10 9 8 7 6 5 4 3 2 1

Printed in Hong Kong

The pictures in this book were done in watercolor and pencil.

Candlewick Press
2067 Massachusetts Avenue
Cambridge, Massachusetts 02140

# A Present for BIG PIG

by
Debi Gliori

illustrated by
Kate Simpson

CANDLEWICK PRESS
CAMBRIDGE, MASSACHUSETTS

It was Big Pig's birthday and
Little Pig had bought her a birthday present.
He had also bought some paper,
some tape, and some ribbon.
Now all he had to do was
wrap the present.

Little Pig folded
the ends of the paper
around the present

and stuck them
down with the tape,
BUT . . .

the tape was *very* sticky
and kept on sticking to Little Pig
instead of the paper.

"I need help," said Little Pig,
and he unstuck himself and took
the very sticky tape, the paper,
the ribbon, and the present
to his wise friend, Owl.

"Please help me wrap
this present for Big Pig's
birthday," said Little Pig.

Owl tore off a strip
of tape,
BUT . . .
it was very tangly,
and it stuck to
Owl's beak.
"Mffffle!" spluttered Owl.

"We need help," said Little Pig,

and he picked up
the tangled dangly owl,
the paper, the ribbon, and the present
and took them all to his big friend, Elephant.

"Please help me unstick Owl and wrap this present for Big Pig's birthday," squeaked Little Pig.

Elephant heaved
and then she tugged
at that awfully dangly,
impossibly tangly,
very sticky tape,
BUT . . .

*RRRrrrip!*
Elephant put her foot
through the paper.

"Oh, dear!" said Elephant.

"Mffffle!" gurgled Owl.

"We need help," said Little Pig,
  and he picked up the tangled dangly
  owl, the ribbon, and the present.

He climbed on Elephant's back and they charged through the forest to find Little Pig's crafty friend, Monkey.

"Please help me untangle Elephant
and unstick Owl and wrap this present
for Big Pig's birthday," cried Little Pig.

But Monkey—naughty Monkey—
snatched the ribbon and tied Elephant,
Owl, and Little Pig together.
Then he ran off giggling.

"Oh, *dear!*" said Elephant.

"MFFFFLE!" blurted Owl.

"We need help," said Little Pig.

So they shuffled and hobbled
down to the river to find Little Pig's
sharp friend, Crocodile.

"Please help me undo this ribbon and
untangle Elephant and unstick Owl and wrap
this present for Big Pig's birthday," squealed Little Pig.
Crocodile bit the ribbon, *snap!* tore off the paper,
*rip!* and dipped Owl in the river, *splosh!*
All the awfully dangly, impossibly tangly,
very sticky tape washed off,
BUT . . .

Little Pig burst into tears.
The paper was torn,
the ribbon was shredded,
and the tape was soggy.
"Now I'll *never* get my
present wrapped," he sobbed.

"I can help,"
said a very little voice.
And from under a leaf
came a tiny spider.
"I may not be wise, or big, or
crafty, or sharp, but I can wrap
anything at all," she said.

Spider whizzed around and around
and up and down and in and out
and round about Big Pig's present
until it was tightly wrapped—
no ribbon, no paper, and no awfully
dangly, impossibly tangly, very
sticky tape, but a beautiful,
silvery, shiny web.

Then Spider, Owl, Crocodile,
Elephant, and Little Pig set off
for Big Pig's birthday party with
the perfectly wrapped present.

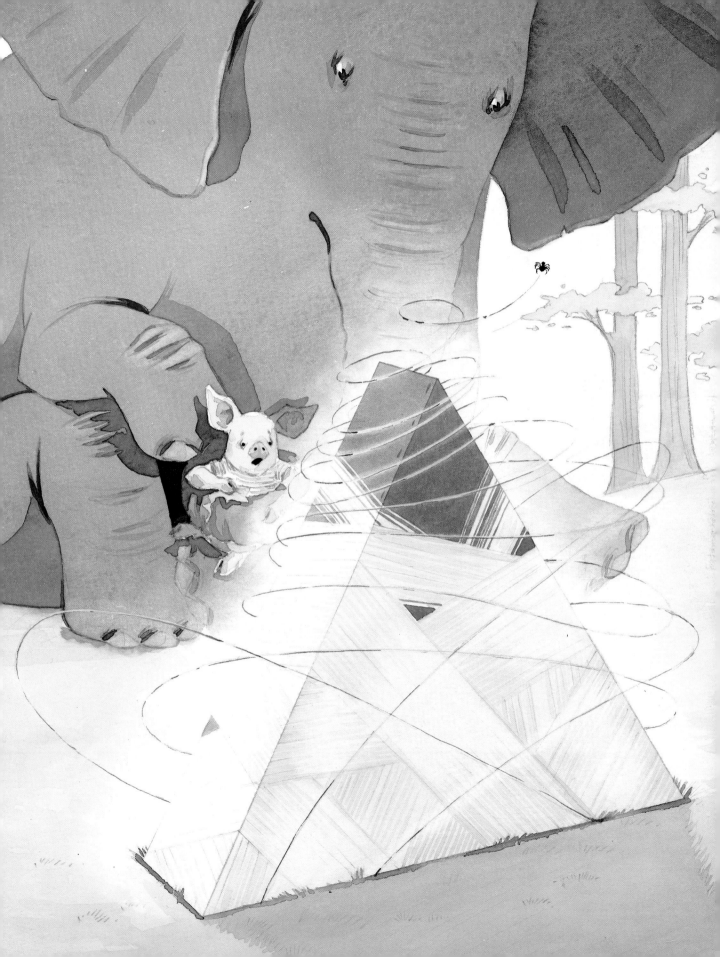

"Why, thank you," said Big Pig,
  tearing the web off in two and a half seconds flat.
"A scooter! What a wonderful present!"

And off she went!

**DEBI GLIORI** lives on a hilltop farm with her husband and two sons in what she describes as "abject poverty, but total bliss." She is also the author and illustrator of *My Little Brother, When I'm Big,* and *New Big House,* as well as the illustrator of David Martin's Lizzie books.

**KATE SIMPSON** earned a degree in graphic design, specializing in illustration. After completing various free-lance projects with educational publishers, she published her first picture book. Kate Simpson lives on a farm and keeps hens, ducks, geese, and sheep.